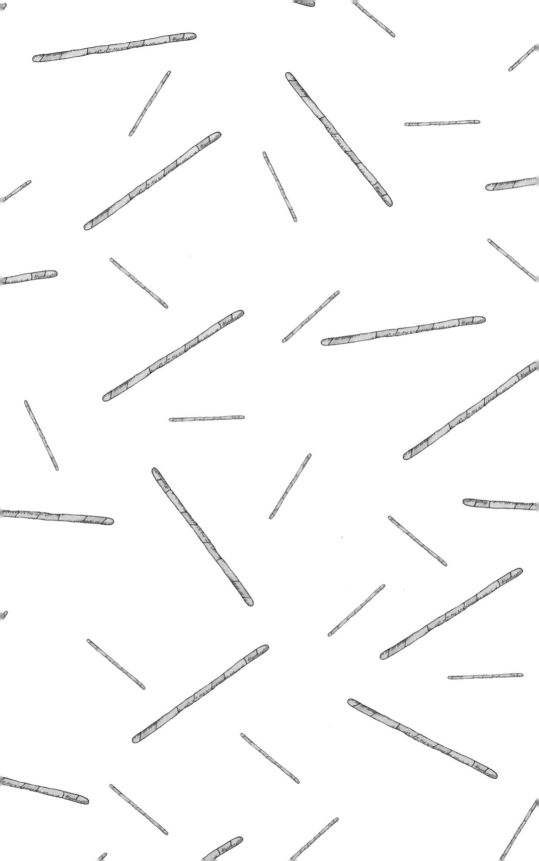

GEORGE AND MARTHA ONE FINE DAY

For my nephew
Alexander Christian Schwartz

The stories in this book were originally published by
Houghton Mifflin Company in *George and Martha: One Fine Day*, 1976.

Houghton Mifflin Books for Children is an imprint of Houghton Mifflin
Harcourt Publishing Company.

www.hmhbooks.com

Library of Congress Cataloging-in-Publication Data is on file.
ISBN 978-0-547-14422-1

Printed in Singapore

TWP 10 9 8 7 6 5 4 3 2 1
4500215190

GEORGE AND MARTHA
ONE FINE DAY

written and illustrated by

JAMES MARSHALL

HOUGHTON MIFFLIN BOOKS FOR CHILDREN
HOUGHTON MIFFLIN HARCOURT
BOSTON • NEW YORK • 2010

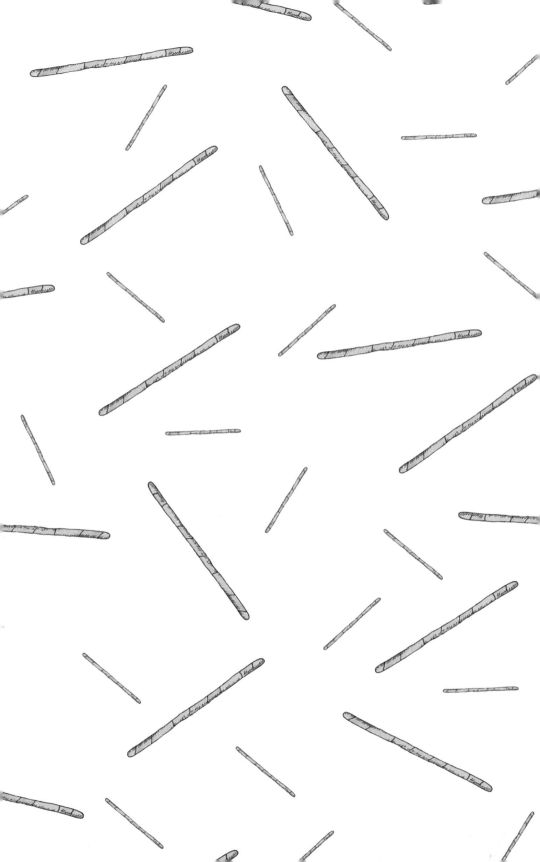

THREE STORIES

ABOUT

TWO BEST FRIENDS

STORY NUMBER ONE

THE TIGHTROPE

One morning when George looked out his window, he could scarcely believe his eyes. Martha was walking a tightrope.

"My stars!" cried George. "I could never do that!"

"Why not?" said Martha. "It's tons of fun."

"But it's so high up," said George.

"Yes," said Martha.

"And it's such a long way down," said George.

"That's very true," said Martha.

"It would be quite a fall," said George.

"I see what you mean," said Martha.

Suddenly Martha felt uncomfortable.
For some reason she had lost all her confidence.
She began to wobble.

George realized his mistake.

Now he had to do some fast talking.

"Of course," he said, "anyone can see you love walking the tightrope."

"Oh, yes?" said Martha.

"Certainly," said George. "And if you love what you do, you'll be very good at it too."

Martha's confidence was restored.

"Watch this!" she said. Martha did some fancy footwork on her tightrope.

STORY NUMBER TWO

THE DIARY

Whenever Martha sat down to write in her diary, George was always nearby.

"Yes, George?" said Martha.

"I was just on my way to the kitchen," said George.

"Hum," said Martha.

Martha decided to finish writing outdoors.
"How peculiar," she said to herself. "I can
still smell George's cologne."
Then Martha heard leaves rustling above
her.

"Aha!" she cried. "You were spying on me!"

"I wanted to see what you were writing in your diary," said George.

"Then you should have asked my permission," said Martha.

"May I peek in your diary?" asked George politely.

"No," said Martha.

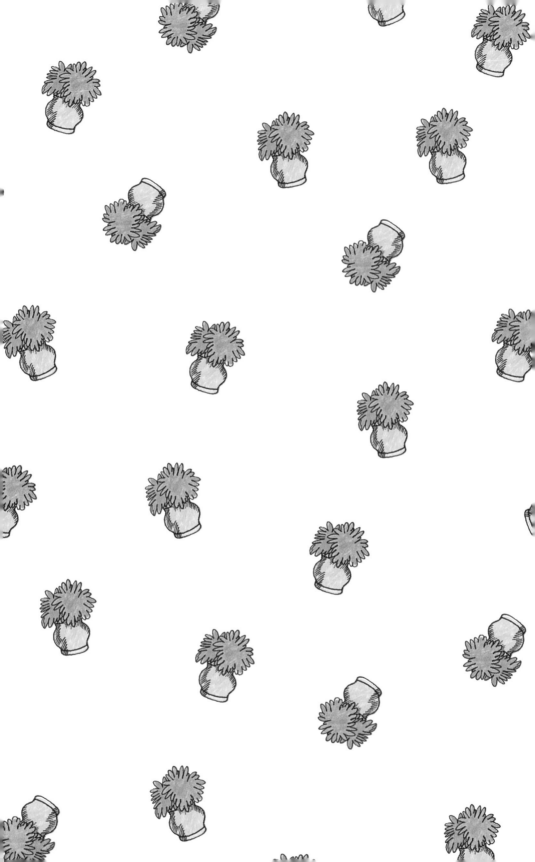

STORY NUMBER THREE

THREE

THE ICKY STORY

At lunch George started to tell an icky story.

Martha strongly objected.

"Please, have some consideration," she said.

But George told his icky story nevertheless.

"You're asking for it," said Martha.

When Martha finished her lunch, she told an icky story. It was so icky that George felt all queasy inside. He couldn't even eat his dessert.

"You're the champ," said George.

"Don't make me do it again," said Martha.

"I won't," said George.

JAMES MARSHALL (1942–1992)

was one of the most popular and celebrated artists in the field of children's literature. Three of his books were selected as New York Times Best Illustrated Books, and he received a Caldecott Honor Award in 1989 for *Goldilocks and the Three Bears*. With more than seventy-five books to his credit, including the popular George and Martha series, Marshall has earned the admiration and love of countless readers.

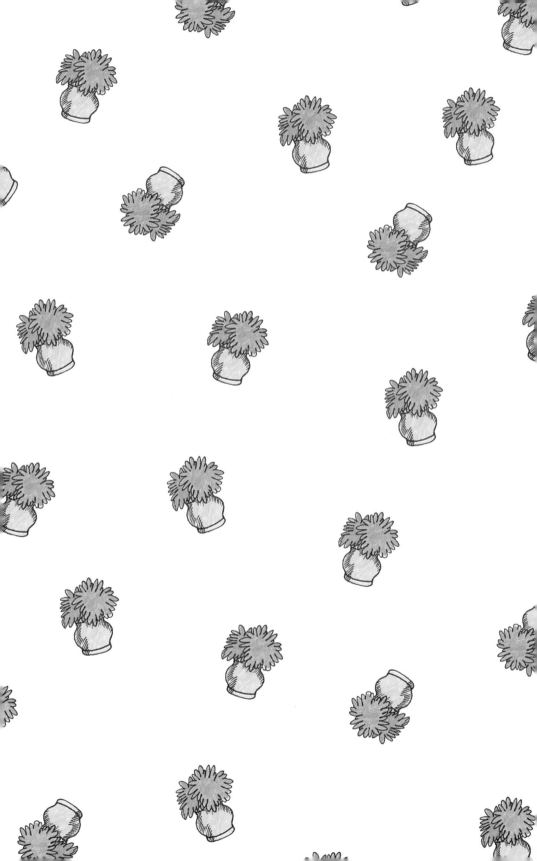